Ladybird books are widely available, but in case of
difficulty may be ordered by post or telephone from:

Ladybird Books – Cash Sales Department
Littlegate Road Paignton Devon TQ3 3BE
Telephone 01803 554761

A catalogue record for this book is available
from the British Library

Published by Ladybird Books Ltd Loughborough Leicestershire UK
LADYBIRD and the device of a Ladybird are trademarks of Ladybird Books Ltd

DISNEY

Lady and the
TRAMP

Ladybird

One Christmas morning, Jim Dear gave his wife, Darling, a very special present. It was wrapped in a box and tied with a pink ribbon.

When Darling opened it, a tiny cocker spaniel puppy peeped out at her.

"How sweet!" cried Darling. "What a perfectly beautiful little lady." And that was how Lady got her name.

Lady loved her new home. She had a big garden to play in and bones to bury. Her best friends, Jock and Trusty, lived nearby. Jock was a small, black Scottish terrier. Trusty was a big, brown bloodhound.

When Lady was six months old,
Darling gave her a smart, blue collar.
The little spaniel rushed off to show
Jock and Trusty.

"My, you're a full grown lady now!"
said Jock.

Lady felt that she was the luckiest,
happiest dog in the whole world.

A few weeks later, Jock and Trusty
found Lady lying by her water bowl.
She looked *very* sad.

"What's wrong, lassie?" asked Jock.

Lady explained that Jim Dear and
Darling seemed cross with her – but
she didn't know why.

"I wouldn'a worry," Jock said.
"Darling is expecting a wee bairn."
Lady looked puzzled.

"He means a baby," explained
Trusty.

"Oh!" said Lady, still puzzled.
"What's a baby?"

"A baby," Jock began, "is a cute little bundle of…" But before he could finish, a voice behind him said, "…trouble."

Lady turned round to see who had
spoken. Walking towards her was
a scruffy but handsome mongrel
called Tramp. "Remember, when a
baby moves in, the dog moves out!"
he warned.

The baby was born that spring. Jim Dear and Darling were overjoyed. And so was Lady.

Sometime later, Jim Dear and Darling went away to visit friends. Aunt Sarah came to look after the baby. She brought her two Siamese cats with her.

The cats were sly and mischievous. They raced through the house frightening the canary, ripping the curtains and upsetting the goldfish bowl!

When Aunt Sarah saw the mess, the cats made it look as though it was all Lady's fault.

Aunt Sarah was very angry. In fact, she decided to buy a muzzle to restrain the little dog. So she took Lady to a pet shop that very day.

As an assistant placed a muzzle over Lady's head, Lady panicked. She managed to wriggle free and leapt off the shop's counter. She ran out of the door into the busy road. Cars and lorries whizzed by.

As she dashed across the road, Lady was nearly knocked down by a car. Terrified, she ran into a side street.

Suddenly, a pack of stray dogs jumped out and began chasing her. Lady fled down an alley to try and escape but a huge fence blocked her way – she was trapped!

Just as the dogs were about to attack
her, Tramp jumped over the fence.
He was a very fierce fighter and
quickly forced the other dogs back
the way they had come. Lady had
been saved!

Tramp walked back to Lady, who was shaking with fear. "Oh! You poor kid," he said, looking at her muzzle. "Come on. We've got to get that thing off."

Tramp led Lady to a nearby zoo where they soon spotted a beaver. He was gnawing through some logs to build a dam.

Tramp persuaded the beaver to use his strong, sharp teeth to bite through Lady's muzzle. In a second, the muzzle dropped off and Lady was free again!

As the stars began to twinkle in the sky, Tramp said, "Come on, it's supper time." He led Lady to the back door of Tony's Italian restaurant.

"Hey, Joe! Look'a who's here!" called Tony to his chef. "Bring them the best'a spaghetti in'a town!"

While Tony and Joe played soft
romantic music, Lady and Tramp
shared a delicious meal.

What a wonderful night, thought
Lady, beginning to chew a strand of
spaghetti. Suddenly, her lips met
Tramp's – they were both eating the
same strand! Lady blushed and the
two dogs gazed dreamily at each
other. They were falling in love.

After supper, Tramp took Lady for a
stroll in a park. As a reminder of the
evening, the two dogs put their paw
prints side by side in some wet
cement. Later that night, they fell
asleep together under the stars.

The next morning, Lady woke with a start. "Oh, dear!" she said, as she suddenly remembered, "I must go home to look after the baby."

Tramp tried to persuade Lady to stay with him but she was determined to go home. Finally, Tramp agreed to show Lady the way back.

As they approached Lady's home, Tramp spotted a hen house. "Ever chased chickens?" he asked Lady.

"Certainly not!" Lady replied.

"Then you've never lived!" cried Tramp. "Follow me!"

Tramp began chasing the chickens around the farmyard. Feathers flew everywhere! Lady was horrified.

Suddenly, there was a gunshot. "Come on!" shouted Tramp as he squeezed under a fence. "That's the signal to get going!"

Tramp and Lady dashed round the corner. They splashed through a stream and jumped over ditches. Tramp was racing ahead. When he turned round, Lady was nowhere to be seen – she had been caught by a dog catcher!

Poor Lady was taken off to the dog
pound – a dark, terrible place where
all the unwanted dogs were locked
up. Lady's eyes filled with tears as
the door of her cell clanged shut
behind her.

Later that day, Lady was surprised to find out that all the other dogs knew about Tramp. It seemed he had lots of other girlfriends. Lady felt sad and disappointed. She had thought she and Tramp had a special friendship. She decided to try to forget him.

Before long, Aunt Sarah came to collect Lady from the dog pound. She was very cross with Lady for running away. When they got home, she chained Lady to a kennel in the garden.

That evening, when Tramp came to visit, Lady refused to speak to him. As Tramp left, Lady felt so unhappy that she lay down in the kennel and cried.

Suddenly, she noticed two eyes glinting in the shadows. A huge rat was scurrying towards the house! Lady barked and tried to chase it away – but her chain held her back.

Luckily, Tramp heard Lady barking. He ran back to see what was wrong.

"It's a rat!" cried Lady. "It ran up the side of the house and into the baby's room." In a flash, Tramp was inside the house, running up the stairs and through the nursery door.

The rat was about to jump into the baby's cot when Tramp leapt at it. The cot toppled over and the baby began to cry. Tramp chased the rat around the room.

There was a terrible fight. Finally,
Tramp trapped the rat and killed it.

Outside, Lady managed to pull free
from her chain. She raced inside the
house and upstairs to the nursery.

But Aunt Sarah had heard the commotion and had come rushing into the nursery. "Merciful heavens!" she cried, staring at the mess.

The dead rat was hidden behind the curtains. Aunt Sarah only saw Lady and Tramp and immediately blamed them.

"You vicious brutes!" she shouted, pushing Tramp into a cupboard with her broom. Then she dragged Lady downstairs and locked her in a dark, damp cellar.

Aunt Sarah telephoned the dog pound and ordered them to come and take Tramp away.

As Tramp was being led to the
pound wagon, Jim Dear and Darling
arrived back home. They rushed
inside the house and were met by
Lady, who had managed to escape
from the cellar.

Lady began barking wildly and led
Jim Dear up to the nursery.

She showed him the dead rat behind
the curtains. Lady knew in her heart
that Jim Dear would understand that
Tramp had killed the rat and saved
the baby.

Meanwhile, Jock and Trusty were following the scent of the pound wagon. They were determined to try and free Tramp.

When they finally caught up with the wagon, Trusty barked at the horses. The horses reared up and the wagon overturned. It crashed to the floor, trapping Trusty's leg beneath. Then the wagon door sprung open and Tramp leapt free.

Suddenly, a taxi drove up with Lady and Jim Dear in it.

Luckily, Jim Dear had realised that Tramp had rescued the baby. From that day, Tramp was welcomed into Jim Dear and Darling's home forever.

*   *   *

A few months later, at Christmas,
Jock and Trusty, whose broken leg
was mending well, came to visit
Lady and Tramp. As they arrived,
four little puppies ran to greet them.

"They've got their mother's eyes,"
said Trusty. He looked fondly at
three of the tiny puppies.

"Aye, but there's a bit of their father in them too," said Jock, trying to stop the fourth puppy chewing his coat!

Behind the puppies sat Lady and Tramp. Tramp looked over at his family and smiled. He knew they would all live happily ever after.

43